This adventure belongs to

To my mom

who gave me magical weapons

and taught me to use them

ISBN 978-1-4521-6989-7

Manufactured in China.

Design by Ryan Hayes.
The illustrations in this book were rendered in goblin blood on sage-blessed papyrus and colored digitally.

10 9 8 7 6 5 4 3 2 1

Chronicle Books LLC
680 Second Street
San Francisco, California 94107

Chronicle Books—we see things differently. Become part of our community at www.chroniclekids.com.

Travis Nichols

chronicle books · san francisco

A Day Like Any Other—HOLD IT.

It's just another normal day. There's absolutely nothing out of the ordinary in your ordinary life in your messy room, and—hey, that's strange . . . that little green door wasn't there yesterday.

So. Here's how this whole thing is gonna work. You, Dear Reader, are going to be guided through words and mazes on a Quest, should you choose to accept it. Most mazes will start with a green arrow pointing into the maze and end with a red one pointing toward an exit. Other instructions will be listed.

And there you have it! Your first task is to find a path through the chaos of your room to that little door marked QO.

Ooh! Elaborate tunnels! Make your way to the Quest Office.

The aged wooden doors to the Quest Office slowly and dramatically creak open. Inside, a super tough-looking warrior/manager shuffles paperwork.

"Ah, greetings. I am Anirak, Firstborn of the Itchy Islands," she says, her voice gravelly with an unplaceable accent. "So, you want to try your hand at being an adventurer, eh? To leave the comforts of home and trudge through the darkest horrors the underworld can conjure and achieve immortal glory in the realm-or-whatever?"

You nod. "Okay," she says. "I suppose you're looking for a proper Quest, then. Let's see . . . no princes or princesses are currently being held captive, so that's out. There haven't been any reports of dragons in a few years. Hmm. Frankly, it's the low season for Questing, so I'm afraid I don't really have anything right now. Unless . . . no, you wouldn't be interested. And, really, I'm not sure you're up for it.

No no no. I'm sorry, that Quest isn't for you. Come back in a few months. Plenty of helpless royals need rescuing in the high season."

You muster your best I'm-not-leaving-without-a-Quest look and aim it squarely at Anirak's left eye—an eye that has seen some things beyond the filing cabinets and stacks of papers in this office. The other eye doesn't see much of anything these days.

Anirak nods. "All right. I'll tell you about this Quest, but honestly, I just don't think you're ready for it. A couple hundred years ago, the Sword of Lacidar was stolen from the Chamber of Priceless and Ridiculously Fantastic Treasures. The thieves quickly realized that they couldn't sell such a famous weapon, so for fear of being caught and thrown into the Forgotten Prison, they broke it into five pieces and hid them around the realm. So, the Board of Directors at the Chamber is offering a sack of gems and various treasures to the adventurer who collects the pieces and returns them so that tourists can ooh and ahh and make big donations at the annual fundraiser.

"But like I said, I don't think this particular Quest is for you. Too treacherous. Too dark and scaaary. Come back later."

If you choose to give up, put down this book and walk away. Ask a teacher or family member to recommend a book about people sitting quietly in a restaurant trying to choose between soup options.

To insist that you're up for the Quest, thrust your fist in the air and yell, "I'm up for it!" Then keep reading.

Anirak smiles slyly. "Fine. Look. I can't promise you'll succeed or survive, but go for it. The first piece of the Sword of Lacidar can be found in the forest just outside of the Quest Office. The others are in Drymouth Desert, inside Shinsplint Mountain, across the Sea of Sickness, and at the top of the Mazing Temple."

She wishes you good luck and sends you on your way.

Hey there. 'Tis your faithful Game Master again. Let's get started.

Here's the inventory of your pack. Dog-ear this page so you can flip back to it quickly. The colored-in stuff is your supplies. The grayed-out stuff is what you should be looking for. Keep track of the things you find by drawing them in. The pieces of the sword are crucial to your Quest. The gems and coins are always good to have. You'll be needing keys eventually, so grab any you see. There are also a couple of items that aren't necessary, but can help you get even more treasure. Ready to go? Remember, the first thing you need is the first piece of the Sword of Lacidar. Go!

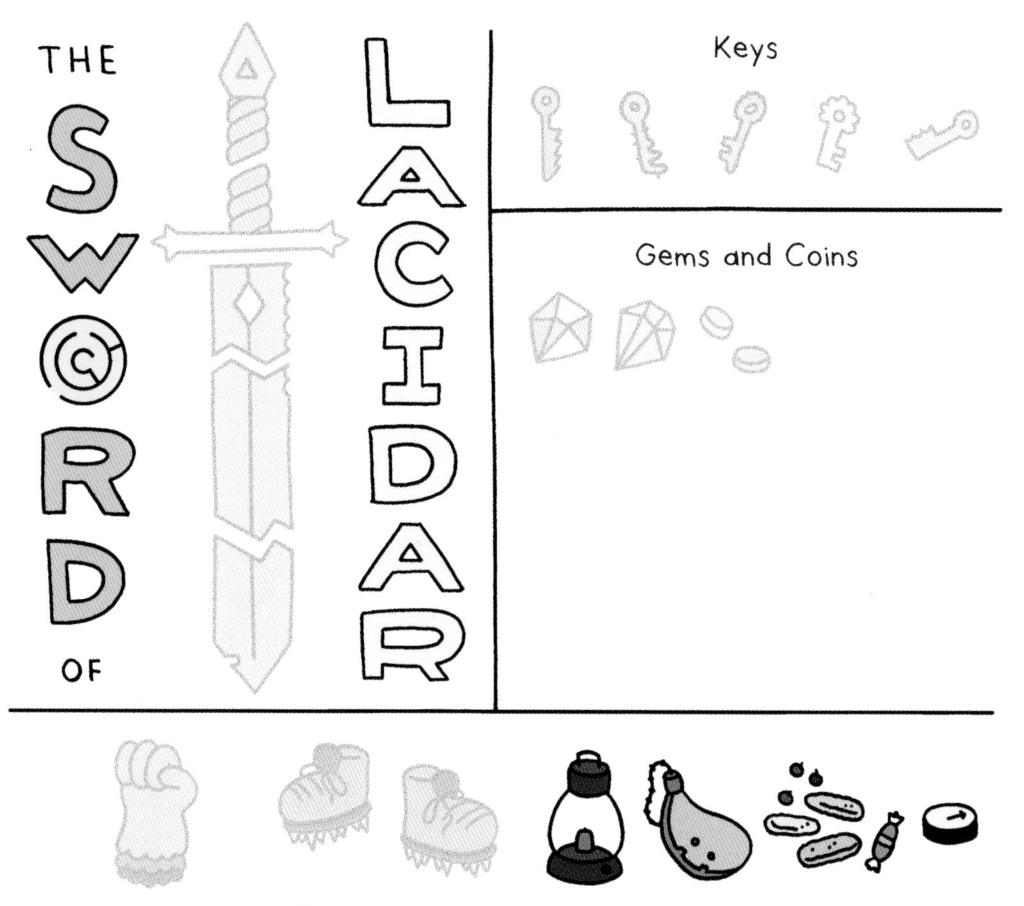

It's getting warmer out. Good thing you dressed in layers. Make sure to snag the green key, and keep an eye out for a legendary gauntlet called the Bronze Fist of Punching. This is the last time I'm going to remind you about those keys, by the way, so keep your eyes peeled.

Ah, there's nothing like wandering through the desert to clear your head. While you're out looking for the second piece of the sword, keep your water bottle full by stopping at five cacti along the way. No more, no less. It would be a shame to get too thirsty so early in your Quest.

Yeesh. Why are there so many bones in this one spot? What could have eaten all of these things? Perhaps we'll never know. By the way, as you make your way through this charming place, keep an eye out for the Spiked Boots of Neverslip. They're not just for looks. The spikes can help you walk across slick, oily surfaces. That might come in handy later on.

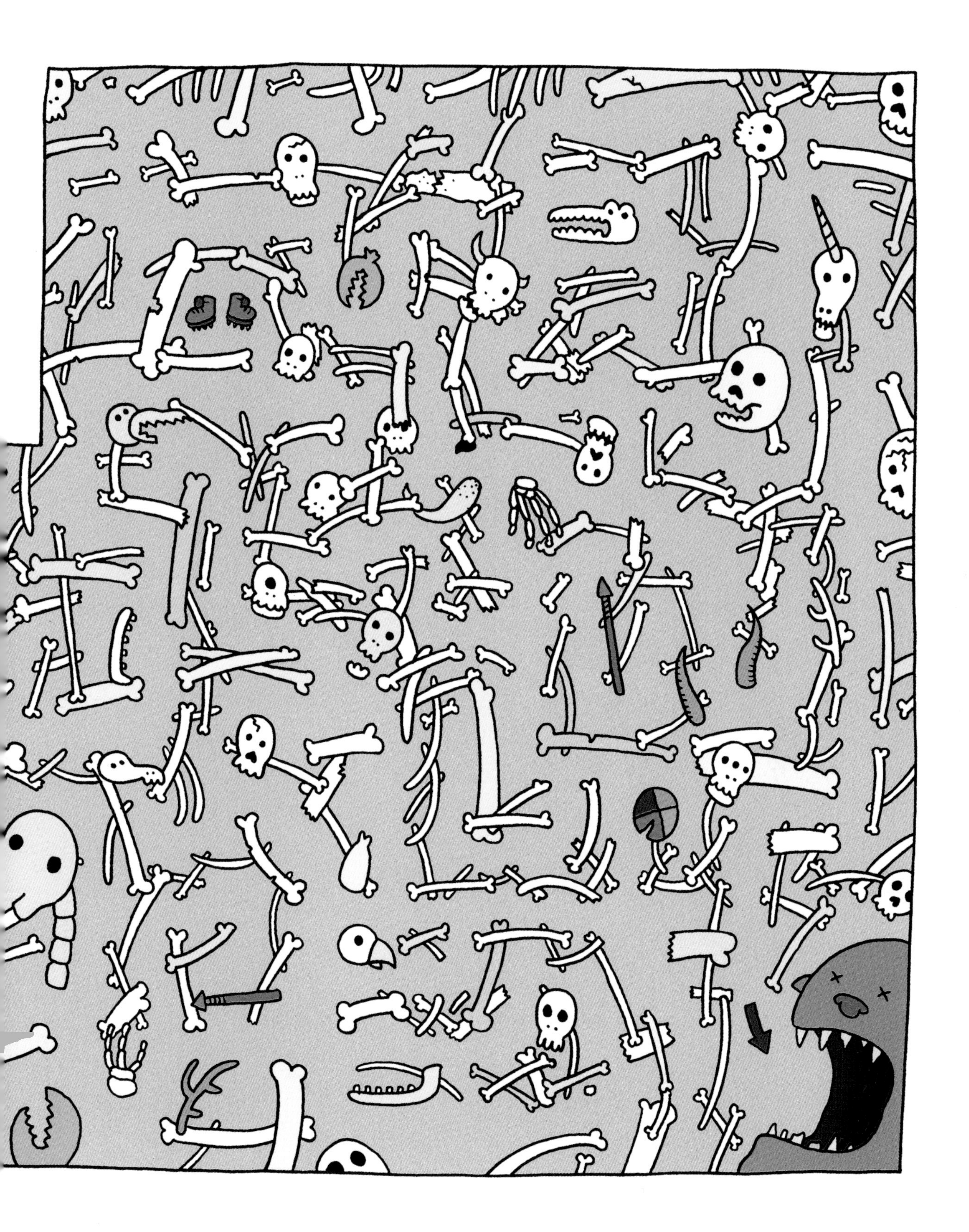

You enter the opening of a cave. Wow, it really stinks in here. And what strange stalactites and stalagmites. Stalactites hang from the ceiling, and stalagmites come up from the ground, by the way. A little rock formation lesson for you. Anyway, they're almost . . . toothy looking. Oh. They are teeth. Okay. This is a giant, dead beast! Get out, quick!

Aaaaand the mouth just shut. I got too caught up in speleology to notice. My fault. Your Game Master has a variety of interests, and I thought you'd like to know. Anyway, you'd better find another way out. Yes. This could get gross really fast.

You've reached the foothills of Shinsplint Mountain. The great mountain looms in the near distance. Hey—what's that piece of paper down there? Grab it before it blows away. And don't disturb the hillbunnies.

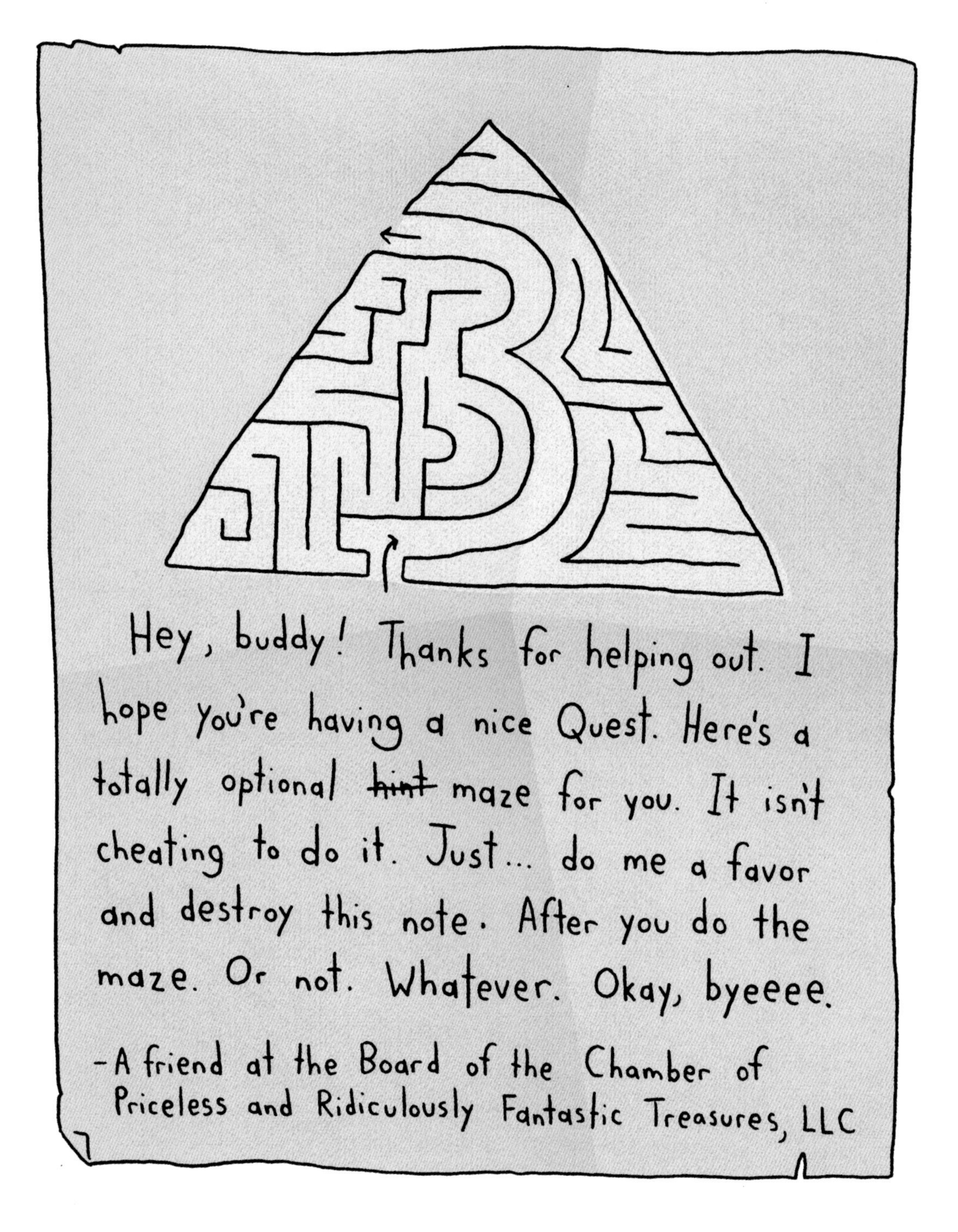

Hey, buddy! Thanks for helping out. I hope you're having a nice Quest. Here's a totally optional ~~hint~~ maze for you. It isn't cheating to do it. Just... do me a favor and destroy this note. After you do the maze. Or not. Whatever. Okay, byeeee.

-A friend at the Board of the Chamber of Priceless and Ridiculously Fantastic Treasures, LLC

At the base of Shinsplint Mountain, you find the entrance to another cave. As you cautiously make sure that you're actually entering a cave and not another giant, dead monster, a robed man emerges from the darkness.

"Hello, adventurer," he says. "I am a monk of the Mazing Temple. First, I just want to say that you're doing a suuuper great job on your Quest. I mean it. But listen. What say we just call it a day here?"

You ask what he means, and he pulls a canvas sack from his robes. "Do you like money? Quit your Quest, go back to your normal life, and this is yours. We can even have a certificate of completion sent to your home."

To quit your Quest, close this book and give it to a friend. They'll perhaps be mildly irritated that you've already drawn in a bunch of the pages, but hey, free book.

To proceed, give the monk a dismissive glance and continue to the next page. Why would he want you to quit? You can handle this.

Gems were once mined in these tunnels, but mostly cleaned out during the Great Gem Rush. If you happen to have a certain Bronze Fist of Punching, there are some soft walls that you can knock down to get to some extra loot. No Bronze Fist of Punching? No loot for you. Make your way to the top. And be careful on those old, rickety ladders, okay?

After climbing the last mineshaft ladder, you turn to discover the last thing you'd expect to see inside a mountain: fields of giant flowers blooming under strange, glowing stalactites. How? Why? What? Who? Huh?

Let's just pause for a moment. Isn't Questing amazing? You get to explore strange new places, witness jaw-dropping sights, and have interesting conversations with colorful characters. And to think—you could have just stayed in your room.

Okay, world. Whaddaya got? Onward!

Well, this is a real puzzler. You'll never guess what's about to happen. The floor is kind of sticky, and there's an enormous hive-looking structure in front of you. There's . . . a faint buzzing coming from inside. You gasp audibly. What could this thing possibly be?

To step through the opening like a brave, curious so-and-so, turn the page.

To abandon your Quest and become a giant flower farmer instead, close this book and go find a nice pair of overalls.

It's a humongous beehive! You can hardly believe it. What a curveball!

The third piece of the Sword of Lacidar is somewhere in this hive, but many paths are blocked by Hexed Bees. Look around for piles of pollen  to collect. Each pile of pollen will let you pass a Hexed Bee.

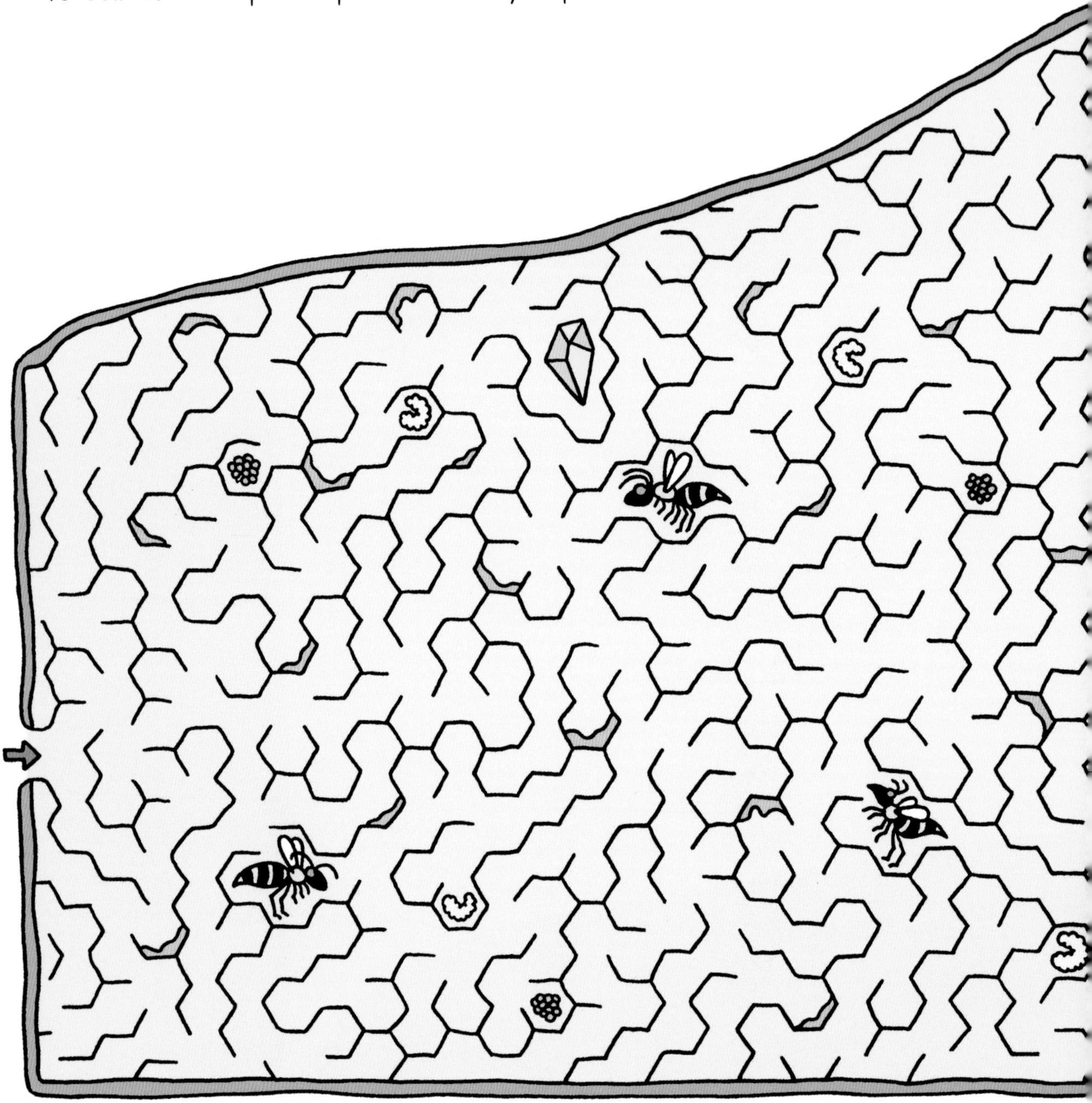

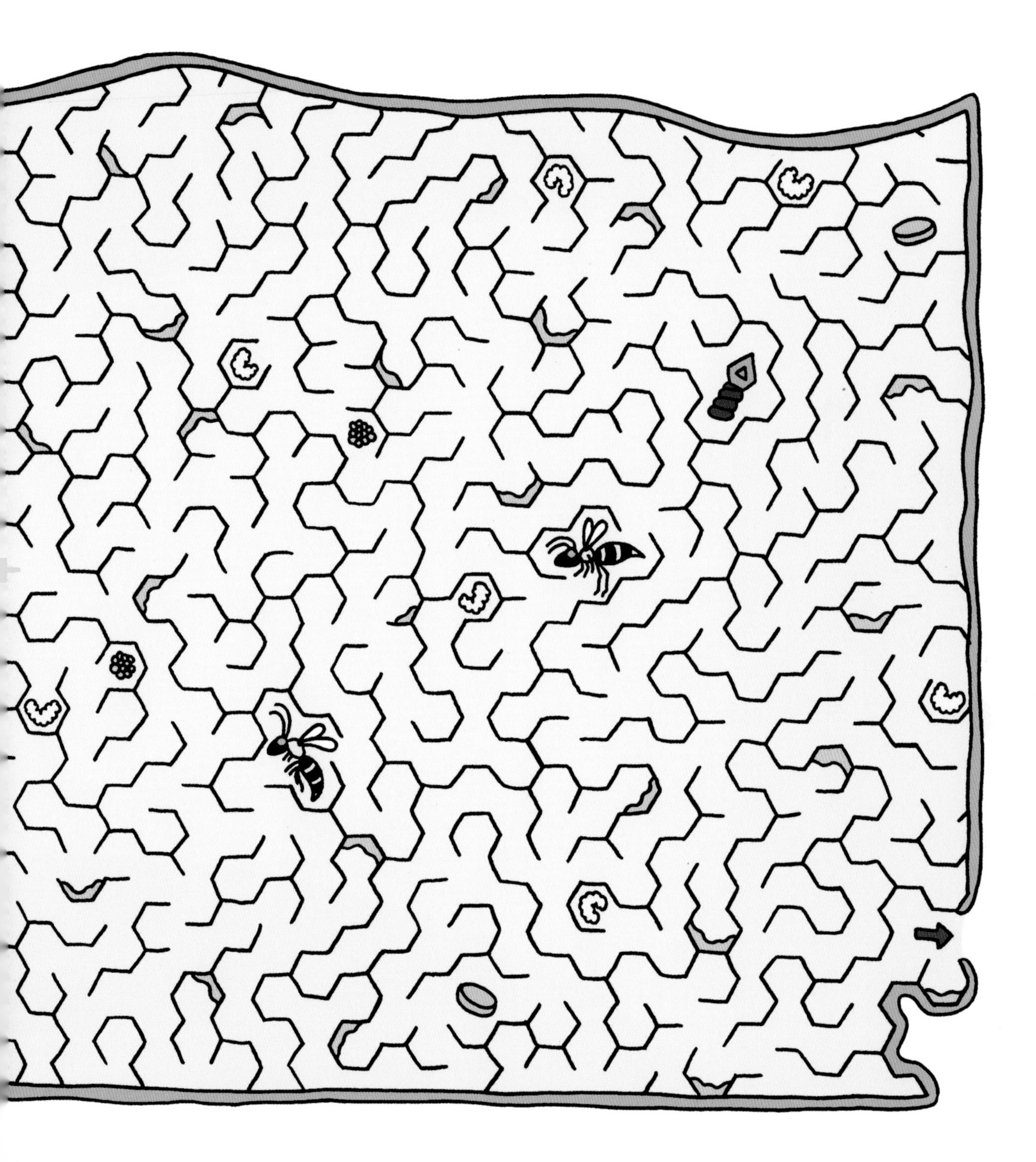

You exit the beehive to find yourself at the peak of Shinsplint Mountain. You can see a coastal village and the Sea of Sickness down below.

Check your inventory for skis or repelling gear. No? Okay then. I guess you're going to be sliding down on your butt. Plot your path and go for it.

At the edge of the village, a colorful character steps into your path, twirling a sparkly walking stick.

"Step right up, adventurer!" they yell. "Play the realm's premier Bonus Game! For the low, low entry fee of five coins, flex your skills and collect as much treasure as you can in one minute."

To play, deduct five coins from your inventory. Then set a timer, watch a clock, or have a friend time you for one minute.

There are a handful of purple, slippery areas that can only be crossed with the Spiked Boots of Neverslip. If you don't have the Spiked Boots of Neverslip, do not step into the slippery areas. A slip and fall while on a Quest is not something that I can be held responsible for. Not again.

START HERE

You continue your path through the coastal village. Your next mission is to cross the Sea of Sickness.

"On a mission to cross the Sea of Sickness, are you?" You turn and see a wizened, hunched old man. His robes smell like fish oil and hot garbage. His breath smells even better. "I reckon you'll be needing a boat, then. Tell you what. You can get whatever you need from my junkyard."

You thank the old man.

"Gimme three gems and four coins. Junk be junk, but junk be my business, friend."

Sheesh, this village is just *money money money* all the time.

Deduct three gems and four coins from your inventory. If you don't have enough loot . . . you've got some back-tracking to do.

Search the junkyard for boat parts. You'll need a hull, mast, sail, rudder, and some rope.

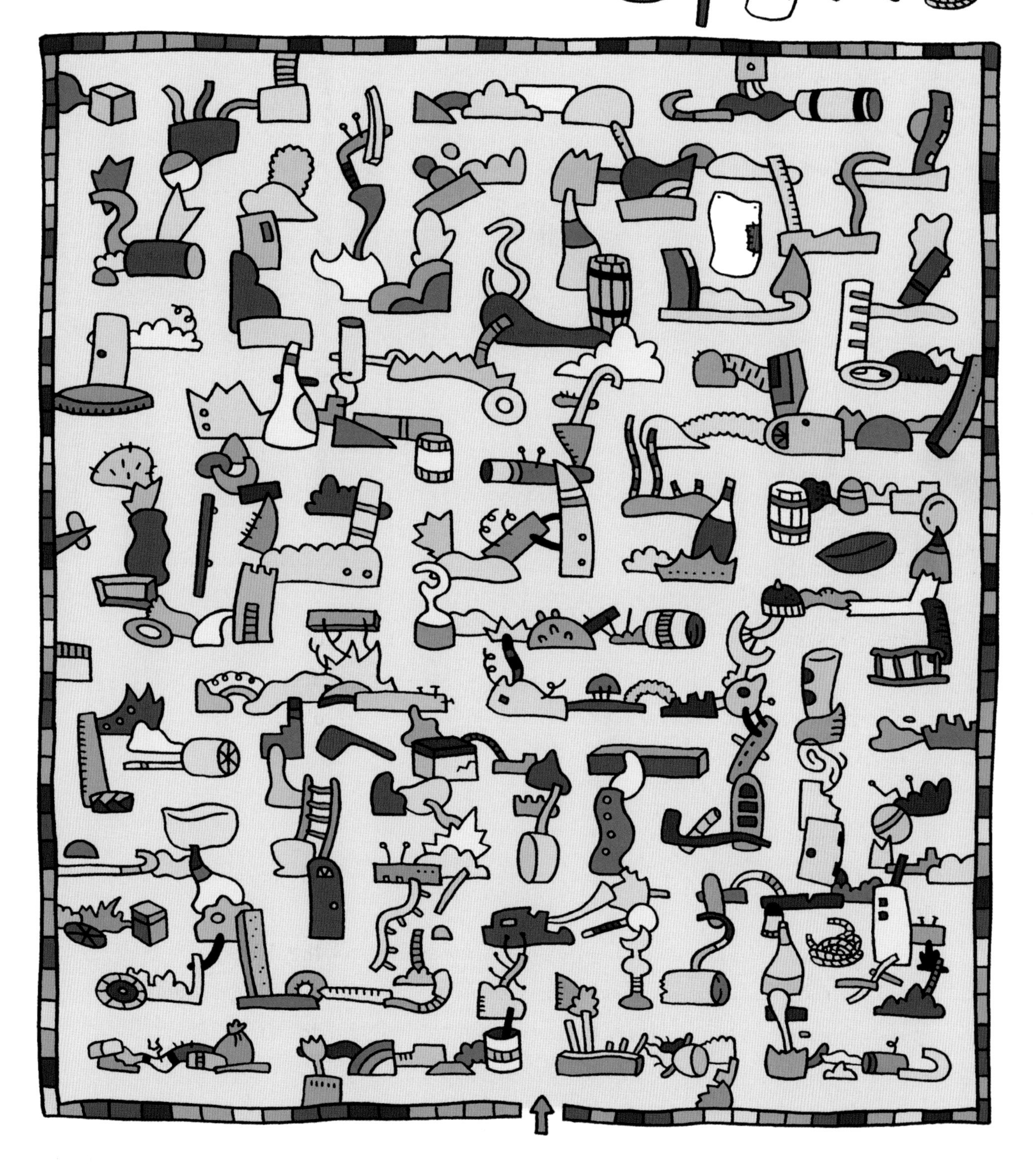

Navigate through the relentless waves of the Sea of Sickness.

You pull your boat to the shore of a small island. A round shack sits in the center. Oh! There's probably a piece of the Sword of Lacidar inside.

You stuff the fourth piece of the Sword of Lacidar in your pack and exit the cottage. Oh, great. One of those pesky monks is sitting at an ice cream cart on the beach.

"So here's a puzzler," she says. "How were simple thieves able to break into the Chamber of Priceless and Ridiculously Fantastic Treasures, steal a sword, break it into five pieces, and hide it all over the realm? Isn't that, you know, somewhat absurd?"

"I'm sure that's an interesting question," you reply. "Two scoops of ragusberry, please."

The monk sighs. "Three copper coins. Free if you stop this silly Quest."

"Here's your money," you say. (Unless you don't want ice cream. But a big part of adventuring is meeting new people and trying local foods. So get some ice cream.)

Subtract three coins from your inventory.

After a quick sail, you reach a series of canals. Seafaring types saunter about singing shanties and moving boxes from here to there and here again. Navigate your boat to a parking spot as inland as you can get.

You hop off your boat and hold up a coin toward a couple of kids playing in the mud. They get it. They'll keep an eye on your boat until you return.

As you leave the fish-smelling canals, you see the Mazing Temple pointing up at the sky. The fifth and final piece of the Sword of Lacidar is at the top. Hopefully there won't be any more of those annoying monks trying to discourage you. What's their deal?

Anyway, the Temple is on the other side of a lovely hedge maze. What? No, you can't just chop your way through it. A bunch of people worked really hard on it. You're going to stroll through the hedge maze and you're going to enjoy it, okay?

The Mazing Temple is vast and smells of incense. Immediately upon entering, you see that you'll be needing some keys. You . . . have been collecting keys along the way, haven't you?

Also, remember, those purple slippery areas can only be crossed with Spiked Boots of Neverslip, and you can only go through those soft walls if you have the Bronze Fist of Punching. If you don't have the necessary items, you can't cross those areas.

At last you have reached the top section of the Mazing Temple. All that stands between you and the final piece of the Sword of Lacidar are a few dozen staircases, ropes, and ladders. Climb, adventurer, climb! But . . . there are three tunnels. Which one do you choose?

You did it! The final piece of the Sword of Lacidar. You arrange the pieces on a large slab of stone. It's super darn beautiful. So, what now? How will you get them to the Board of Directors at the Chamber of Priceless and Ridiculously Fantastic Treasures? Think they'd offer you a free museum membership and a discount at the café? Museum cafés can be pretty pricey, you know.

Anyway, you can sort that out once you get back. So . . . is there a Pegasus or something you can hop on to get back quickly, or are you going to have to go all the way back through the mazes again (fine, maybe you could hack down a few hedge walls this time), or—

Suddenly, a figure looms over the table and the sword pieces. You look up and see—well, how to put this delicately—not exactly a handsome fellow. He has pink, puffy eyelids under yellow eyes, greasy black hair, and a long, gray robe. Now now, don't jump to conclusions and assume he's evil just because he's hideous.

"Greetings, adventurer!" His voice creaks like rusted metal. "I am Gnik Luohg, a proud representative of the Board of Directors at the Chamber of Priceless and Ridiculously Fantastic Treasures." He holds out an ID card. It's laminated, so he must be the real deal.

"Congratulations on completing your Quest! As promised, I have a bag of gems for you as a reward." His right eye, the slightly grosser one, twitches. He begins snatching up the pieces. As they touch, they sparkle and sizzle. "Now . . . the Sword of Lacidar . . . is . . . mmmmiiiiiine."

In a flash of smoky-blue light, Gnik Luohg twists and contorts. He pulls a gray, rusted, bony crown from deep inside his mouth (gross!) and places it atop his lengthening, greasy locks. He is slightly more hunched and grotesque than before, and has a new beard that most likely smells terrible. Oh, that's pretty neat—you notice that the little buttons on his robe have changed somewhat.

"Fool!" he bellows, his voice less strained for lack of a crown down his throat. "Behold my true form! Check out these spooky bone-shaped buttons! Right? Fear me! I am the Ghoul King, and you have sealed the fate of this realm for ten thousand years! BWAHAHA!"

The pieces of the sword pop and smolder in his hands. "Can you recommend a good blacksmith?" he asks mockingly.

As the Ghoul King continues to laugh at his wicked success, you realize that your natural adventuring skills have been taken advantage of. You completely fell for it. Is the Chamber of Priceless and Ridiculously Fantastic Treasures even a real museum? Dang. It sounded like a really fun place.

Suddenly, something catches your eye.

A large stone behind the Ghoul King slides away silently, and three Mazing Monks leap from inside the Temple, grab the Ghoul King's arms, and wrestle the pieces of the Sword from his grip. They thrust them into your pack, and one of them yells, "Quick! Run!"

As you slide down the back wall of the Temple, three thoughts race through your mind: 1) The monks were on your side all along! 2) This is super exciting. 3) Way to not be prejudiced back there about Gnik Luohg / the Ghoul King. Good for you, adventurer!

Escape the Ghoul King through the Ruined City! Go!

You must hide the Sword of Lacidar more deeply than before. Take once piece to each of the three waiting Monks from the Mazing Temple, then find the exit.

The exit takes you to the Useless Bridges of Wasted Rock.

As you pass under the last Useless Bridge, a Mazing Monk you've never seen before removes the fourth piece of the Sword of Lacidar from your pack. You reach to hand her the fifth piece, but she stops you.

"Nay," she says. "Hold on to that final piece, adventurer. That is for you to hide yourself, one way or another."

You ask the Monk why you were allowed to collect the pieces of the Sword of Lacidar only to have to hide them again.

"Finding that which is hidden is the heart of any Great Adventure," she says. "And it's good to stretch your legs once in a while. Follow me."

The Mazing Monk leads you to the mouth of a cave. Yes, another cave. Last one, I promise. She pauses in front of a well.

"You have two choices, adventurer. You may drop the final piece of the sword down into this wishing well. Do this, and your Quest is over. You'll awaken and find yourself back in your normal life. Your other choice is to go deeper. Take the last piece of the sword with you through these tunnels and out into adventures that you cannot even begin to fathom. Either way, you have succeeded, and we Monks of the Mazing Temple are quite impressed with you. Now. What is your choice, adventurer?"

To stop your Quest here, drop the sword piece in the well, put this book down, and see if there are any chores you need to do.

To go deeper, continue to the next page and beyond. Prepare for one of those epic endings that feels like a whole new beginning. Ooooh!